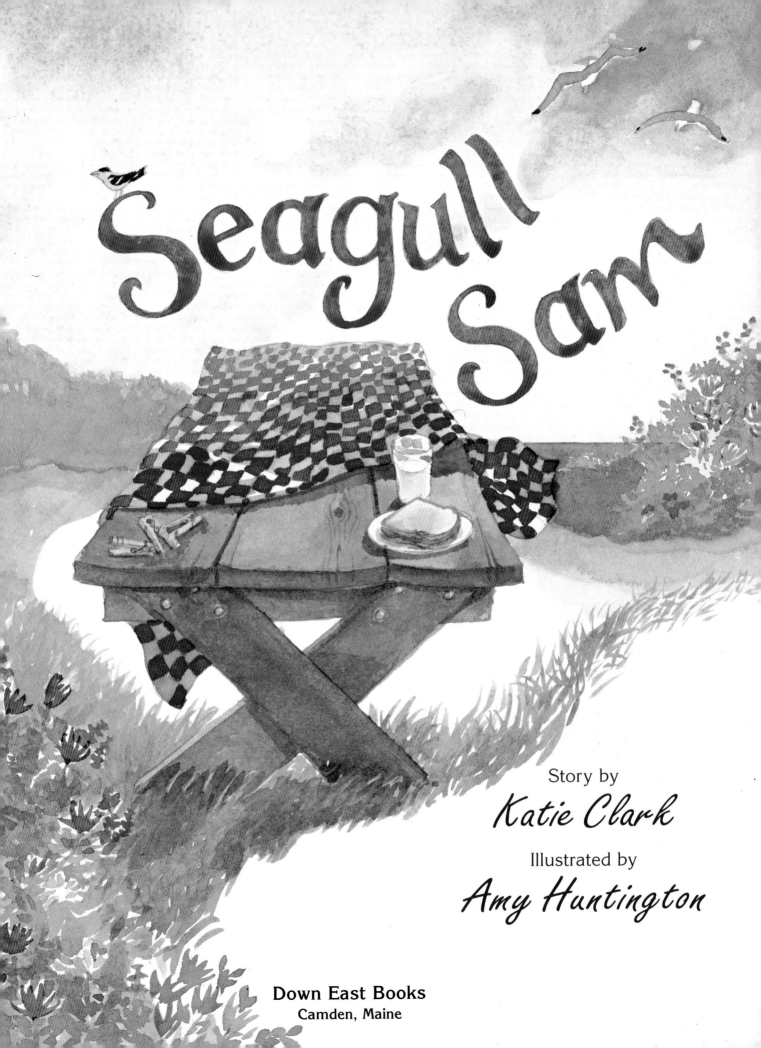

Seagull Sam

Story by
Katie Clark

Illustrated by
Amy Huntington

Down East Books
Camden, Maine

Printed in China

2 4 5 3 1

Down East Books
a division of Down East Enterprise
Book Orders: 800-685-7962
www.downeastbooks.com
Distributed to the trade by National Book Network

Library of Congress Cataloging-in-Publication Data

Clark, Katie, 1962-
    Seagull Sam / story by Katie Clark ; illustrated by
Amy Huntington.
       p. cm.
    Summary: When Sam's brother and sister will not
let him fly kites with them, Sam finds with the help of
a large white shirt, some seagulls, and a strong wind
he can do amazing things.
    ISBN-13: 978-0-89272-715-5 (trade hardcover :
alk. paper)
    [1. Brothers and sisters--Fiction. 2. Kites--Fiction.
3. Gulls--Fiction.]
    I. Huntington, Amy, ill. II. Title.
PZ7.C54823Se 2007
[E]--dc22
                                        2006028692

Dedication:

To my mother,
and sisters and brothers
everywhere, including
my own: Fiona, Phebe and
Lloyd.

–K.C.

For Patrick.

–A.H.

Sam was too small to fly kites with his brother and sister.

"The wind is so strong," said Caroline, "you'll just
get dragged along the ground."

"You might get hurt," said Jonathan.

They made him sit on the back steps,
so he wouldn't be in the way.

"It's not fair," said Sam. But Jonathan just turned away.
He ran into the wind, tugging his kite high in the air.

"It's up! It's up!" he yelled. The fiery breath of
the dragon kite flamed red against the blue sky.

"My turn!" hollered Caroline.
She ran across the grass, letting the string unroll in her hands.
The prancing unicorn leapt above the trees.

"Look! My unicorn is flying!" she cried. "Oh, look!"

But Sam would not look.
At least not at the kites soaring above his head.
He looked at the ant crawling across his toes.
He looked at the laundry blowing in the wind.
He looked at the seagulls pecking
in the cracks of the picnic table.

"Silly birds," scoffed Sam. "You're always eating.
Eating! Eating! Eating!"

"Why don't you fly?" he scolded. With a sudden burst, Sam
rushed at the gulls, beating his arms wildly up and down.

"Aark! Aark!" he cried.

One seagull hopped sideways, then flapped into the air.

"Who needs to fly a kite anyway," cried Sam, "when you can fly like a seagull?"

He jumped over the flower bed.

He swooped around the apple tree and over to the clothesline.

Sam tugged hard at the largest, whitest shirt.

He buttoned up the front,
but let the sleeves hang loose.

"Aark!" Sam squawked. "Aark!" He rushed toward the picnic table. The second seagull took to the air with a swift thump of its wings.

Sam pretended to peck in the cracks. "Aark! Yum-yum. Aark!"

Standing tall, he tipped his head toward the sun.

"I'm like you!" Sam called to the birds circling high overhead. "I'm a seagull!"

The wind whistled through his hair.
It buffeted the shirt sleeves and spread the tails like a sail.

Sam leaned forward, just as his toes lifted from the table.

SAM
WAS
FLYING!

Out of the corner of his eye, he saw the seagulls lifting higher in the sky.

"Wait for me," cried Sam. "I'm coming!"

He held his arms wide and tried to copy the movements of the birds.
Arch . . . and pump . . . and soar.

The gulls banked slightly then flew over the tall
pine tree toward the ocean.

Sam followed.

Everything looked small.
Sam's house.   The cars along the road.   The boat at the dock.

"I'm so BIG!" shouted Sam.

He followed the seagulls in a wide arc out over the ocean.
        Far below, he saw the beach, the piney island,
                and three tiny lobster boats bobbing in the surf.

Riding the wind back to the shoreline,
   Sam dipped and swooped above the road to town.

"I can see the church steeple and the gas station sign and the
   flagpole and all the roofs of all of the houses!" cried Sam.

"I can see everything!" He pumped his arms hard and leaned.
   "Come on, seagulls! I'll race you home again!"

Flying toward his own rooftop,
        Sam heard the faint call of his name.

Below, he saw two little figures running here and there
        around the house and across the yard.

Two bright spots of color shone in the grass:
        one of red and purple,
                the other of gold and white.

"The kites," he whispered. "They crashed."

Sam circled his house.
He watched the seagulls again.
They cupped their wings slightly and slowed.
Sam did the same.

But just above the apple tree, the birds gave a sudden flap
of their wings and lifted back up and out toward the ocean.

"Good-bye!" called Sam. "Good-bye!"

And he landed, feet first in the grass.   Flutter.   Thump.

"How'd you do that, Sam?" cried Jonathan.

"Let me try!" demanded Caroline.

Sam looked into the eager faces of his brother and sister.
Far above them, two white dots shimmered in the blue, blue sky.

"I'm sorry," he said slowly.
         "But you are too big.
              You might get dragged on the ground.
                  You might get hurt."

Sam unbuttoned the shirt and tucked it under his arm.
He let the screen door slam behind him.

In the kitchen, he got out a loaf of bread,
a jar of peanut butter, and a knife.
"No wonder seagulls are always eating," he muttered.
"Flying sure makes you hungry."

"Aark." A thin faraway call swept in on the wind.
"Aark . . . aark . . . ."

Sam gazed out the window as he took a bite of his sandwich.
"But I think I'll just eat half," he said to himself.
"I wouldn't want to get too big too quickly."

Tomorrow was supposed to be
another wonderfully windy day.